A Bad Case of
GHOSTS

Kenneth Oppel

Illustrated by
Sam Sisco

MONTEREY COUNTY
SALINAS
CALIFORNIA
LIBRARIES

WITHDRAWN

CS
W9-CQO-446

A
LITTLE APPLE
PAPERBACK

SCHOLASTIC INC.

New York   Toronto   London   Auckland   Sydney
Mexico City   New Delhi   Hong Kong   Buenos Aires

For Lloyd

If you purchased this book without a cover, you should be aware that this book is stolen property. It was reported as "unsold and destroyed" to the publisher, and neither the author nor the publisher has received any payment for this "stripped book."

No part of this publication may be reproduced in whole or in part, or stored in a retrieval system, or transmitted in any form or by any means, electronic, mechanical, photocopying, recording, or otherwise, without written permission of the publisher. For information regarding permission, write to Scholastic Canada Ltd., 175 Hillmount Rd., Markham, Ontario, Canada L6C 17Z.

ISBN 0-439-30341-9

Text copyright © 1994, 2000 by Kenneth Oppel.

All rights reserved. Published by Scholastic Inc., 555 Broadway, New York, NY 10012, by arrangement with Scholastic Canada Ltd. SCHOLASTIC, LITTLE APPLE PAPERBACKS, and associated logos are trademarks and/or registered trademarks of Scholastic Inc.

12 11 10 9 8 7 6 5 4 3 2 1   1 2 3 4 5 6/0

Printed in the U.S.A.   40
First Scholastic printing, December 2001

Contents

Chapter 1

Spooked

GILES BARNES couldn't sleep.

He sat up in bed, hugging a pillow to his chest, and looked around the dark room. There was hardly anything in it. The moving van had arrived very late and there hadn't been much time to unpack. Apart from his bed, the only other things in the room were cardboard crates and bits of furniture pushed against the walls. Pale light from the street seeped through the grimy window and cast weird, dinosaur-shaped shadows across the empty room.

He didn't like this new house of theirs. From the moment he'd set foot inside, he'd felt there was something dark and sad about it. Plaster was flaking off the ceilings in big patches, the wallpaper was droopy, the doors hung crookedly on their hinges, and the creaky wood floors had splinters in them. There was a funny smell to the house, too, which reminded him of his grandma's dark and unfriendly root cellar.

"It's a great old house," his father had said enthusiastically when they arrived. "It's just been shut tight for a long time. All it needs is a good airing out. And a little fixing up."

"And a lot of fixing up," said his mother, showing him the doorknob that had just pulled off in her hand.

"I wish we were back in our old place," Giles grumbled to himself in bed. He'd had to say goodbye to Jim and David, his best friends, and now there was a whole summer to get through without knowing anyone. He didn't understand why they'd had to move at all. What was wrong with their old house? It was a lot better than this ancient thing — he'd be surprised if it didn't fall to pieces before the end of the week!

A shadow shaped like a Triceratops moved across the wall and Giles shuddered. It's just a car

going by outside, he told himself. You have an overactive imagination. Mom's always saying so.

But a sudden creak sent a little ripple of electricity up and down his neck.

It's just the floors, he told himself, trying to sound sensible like his mother. Old houses make lots of strange noises. There's nothing to be afraid of.

The radiator clanked and Giles jumped.

"This is ridiculous," he said. "I'm going to sleep."

But his eyes were closed for only a few seconds before he heard a strange rustling sound in the room. He popped open his eyes. It was coming from the corner by the window. No, it was closer to the door . . . no, it was up near the ceiling, then off to the right of the bed. This weird, whispery fluttering noise seemed to be moving!

Giles was starting to get freaked out. He'd had it with moving shadows and strange noises. He jumped out of bed and switched on the light. The noise stopped. All the monstrous shadows evaporated. It was just like his mother was always telling him. Turn on the lights, the noises always stop. Giles took a good look around his room, then flicked off the light, dived back into bed, and pulled the covers up to his ears.

There was some more creaking, but he didn't let it bother him. Besides, he was getting too drowsy to care anymore. Soon he was fast asleep.

Chapter 2

The Quarks

THE NEXT MORNING, Giles started unpacking his things. First, he set up his desk and shelves. That helped — already the room was beginning to look a little nicer, more like home. He wasn't crazy about the wallpaper, which was a dingy, grayish color with a faded pattern of vines and ivy leaves. He stuck up some of his favorite posters with putty.

The window was so dirty he could barely see out. He asked his dad for a cloth and some glass cleaner and gave the glass a good scrub. It was a sunny summer day, and there were lots of people on the sidewalks. He could see an old man leaning on a walker, making his way slowly past their house.

Across the street was a small park. Giles squinted. Weird!

Perched on the monkey bars were a boy and a girl. That wasn't weird. It was what they were wearing. They both wore enormous sets of head-phones that were plugged into a large machine the girl carried around her neck on a thick strap. And they were both looking straight at his house!

As Giles watched, the girl twiddled a few knobs on the machine and then said something to the boy. They climbed down from the monkey bars, crossed the street, and stood on the sidewalk, staring intently at the house.

Giles could see them more clearly now. He guessed that they were about his age. The girl was very tiny, with small, thin hands, pale skin, and two precise blond braids dangling on either side of her head. The boy had tightly curled red hair, and his broad face was splotched with freckles.

But what were they doing with that machine?

The girl said something to the boy, but he obviously didn't hear her. She knocked on his head with her knuckles to get his attention. They had a short conversation.

Then, as Giles watched in amazement, they

actually walked through the front gate of the house and into the garden! They stood on the lawn, listening to their headphones again, and the girl was now scribbling in a notepad.

What on earth?

Giles couldn't control his curiosity any longer. He went downstairs, opened the front door, and walked out. The boy and girl didn't seem to notice him.

"Hello," he said uncertainly.

No response.

"Hey," he said, more loudly.

They both jumped and yanked off their headphones.

"Hi," said the boy with the red hair. "Do you live here?"

"We just moved in," Giles told him.

The boy and girl looked at each other in surprise.

"Oh," said the boy. "We thought it was still empty. I'm Kevin Quark, and this is my older sister, Tina. We're geniuses."

Giles blinked.

"Kevin," said the tiny girl, "be quiet."

"Well, it's true, isn't it?"

"Of course, but it's not the kind of thing you tell people when you first meet them, is it?"

Kevin smiled cheerfully. "Oh well," he said. "So, what's your name?"

"Giles Barnes."

"Are you a genius?"

"I've never really thought about it," Giles replied.

"Well, it's usually pretty obvious," Kevin told him. "Can you name all the capital cities of Europe? Do you get 10 out of 10 on all your class quizzes? Can you do the thirteen-times table in your head? Those are some of the first signs."

Giles felt out of breath just listening to Kevin.

"We've counted the number of bricks in our house and calculated the amount of water that flushes through the toilet every day. Sometimes we invent things — Tina's brilliant at that. She knows everything about chemistry and electricity. She can make liquid in a test tube turn blue and then explode! She can make sparks sizzle between two rods!"

Tina stood there silently, smiling faintly.

"Well, I don't think I'm genius material, compared to all that," Giles admitted.

10

"Well, that's all right," said Kevin good-naturedly. "I'm only a little bit of a genius myself. Now, Tina, she's a vast genius. She's the brains behind the whole operation. The ghostometer was her idea."

Tina nudged her brother in the ribs with her elbow.

"Owww!" Kevin cried out. "What was that for?"

"For telling him about the ghostometer."

"The what?" Giles asked.

Tina sighed. "The ghostometer," she said. "It detects ghosts."

Giles took a good look at the contraption around her neck. It looked like a toaster with lots of switches and knobs added on.

"That thing detects ghosts?" he said. "You're not serious!"

"I'm completely serious," said the tiny girl. "I'll admit, it does need some minor readjustments. But I'll have you know that we got some very strong readings from your house."

"Did we?" Kevin asked.

Tina rolled her eyes. "Yes, Kevin, we did. Weren't you listening?"

"Sometimes it all sounds the same to me. All those little beeps and blerps."

"They were positive readings," Tina said, exasperated.

"But didn't we get positive readings from Tom's dog once?" Kevin asked politely.

Tina went red in the face. "Yes, but that was in the early stages. It's much more reliable now."

"Hang on a second," said Giles. "You think my house is haunted?"

"It's possible," said Tina gravely.

"I don't believe in ghosts," Giles said firmly, trying to sound like his mother.

"Are you sure you haven't seen anything spooky or creepy or basically weird in there?" Kevin wanted to know.

"No," said Giles quickly, "absolutely not."

He couldn't help thinking about the strange noises he'd heard in his room last night. But that was just his imagination. It had nothing whatsoever to do with ghosts.

"Well," said Kevin eagerly, "no one's lived in this house for years. I bet it's haunted. They say a crazy lady used to live here. She never left the house. There's bound to be ghosts coming out of every nook and cranny!"

"Kevin, please," said Tina in a tired voice, "this

12

is all very unscientific. We haven't proven anything yet."

Giles took a look at his house. Now that he thought about it, it did look a little haunted. He felt a tingling at the base of his skull. Had a crazy lady really lived here? Could there really be ghosts?

"Well, look," said Tina, "we've got to do some work on the ghostometer."

"And if anything zany happens," said Kevin hopefully, "give us a call and we'll be right over. Here's our card."

"Good-bye," said Giles, feeling slightly over-whelmed. He looked at the business card Kevin put in his hand. It said:

Tina and Kevin Quark.
Local Geniuses.
Capable of just about everything.
Reasonable Rates.

"I've never met geniuses before," Giles mumbled, going inside.

Chapter 3

Haunted

"I MET SOME KIDS who said this house is haunted," Giles told his parents at lunch.

"There's no such thing as ghosts," Mrs. Barnes said with a smile. Mrs. Barnes was a professor of mathematics at the university. She liked numbers, she liked long equations, she liked things you could solve on paper. She did not believe in ghosts.

"Aunt Lillian believes in ghosts," Giles pointed out.

"Yes, well, Aunt Lillian believes in quite a few weird things," said Mrs. Barnes.

Giles liked Aunt Lillian, no matter what his Mom said. Aunt Lillian dressed like a gypsy, with scarves and headbands and too much makeup. She always told ghost stories when she visited.

"Dad, do you believe in ghosts?" Giles asked.

"Well, I'm not sure," said his father. "I've certainly never seen a ghost."

"There you go," said Mrs. Barnes. "No one I know has ever seen a ghost. That's because they're not real."

"But there are lots of things we haven't seen that we know are real," said Giles.

"Like what?" Mrs. Barnes asked.

"Like . . . like atoms!" said Giles.

"Ah, well, that's different," said Mrs. Barnes. "That's science."

"They said a crazy woman used to live here."

"Oh, please," said Mrs. Barnes.

"Don't you like the house, Giles?" his father asked.

"It's a little creepy," said Giles.

"It's just an old house, that's all," said Mr. Barnes. "Once we get it all fixed up, you won't think it's so bad."

Giles's father was right. After a few days, he'd almost forgotten about the Quarks and their stories about ghosts and crazy ladies. The house

15

was getting more and more cheerful as they arranged their furniture and brought in plants and put up paintings. Mr. Barnes was even giving the house a fresh coat of paint on the outside, and he promised to get new wallpaper for Giles's bed-room.

"This house isn't so bad after all," Giles said to himself. He was in his bedroom, working on a model airplane. The sun and the smell of summer were streaming through his window and he was just about to glue a particularly delicate bit of his model together . . . when he heard it.

He put down his model and listened. There it was again, slightly louder now, that same whis-pery rustle he'd heard the very first night! He held his breath. If he hadn't known any better, he'd have said it sounded like a bird flapping its wings.

It was bright daylight, and Giles didn't feel very frightened at all; in fact, he felt curious. He stood up and walked to his window. Poking out his head, he peered under the eaves. In their old house, some birds had built their nests there, and he'd been able to hear them fluttering around under the roof. But there was nothing to see here — no birds, no nests.

He ducked his head back through the window. He could still hear it! How bizarre. It sounded almost as if a bird were soaring around his bedroom, because the sound was definitely moving, swooping from one corner of his room to the next. But he couldn't see anything!

Now Giles was starting to get nervous. He was all alone in the house. His parents had gone downtown to see about some curtains and wouldn't be home for at least an hour.

Stay calm, he told himself. There must be a perfectly reasonable explanation for all this. What would Mom do if she were here?

Then, all of a sudden —

"Hello!"

The hair on the back of Giles's neck stood up. It was a woman's voice, and it had come from right beside his ear! But there was nothing to be seen!

"Hello, hello!"

That did it! He lunged for his desk and rummaged frantically through his drawers until he found the Quarks' business card. Then he slammed the bedroom door behind him, raced to the downstairs phone, and punched in the number with a shaking finger.

"Kevin and Tina Quark, local geniuses. May I help you?"

"Kevin," said Giles, recognizing the voice at the other end of the line, "it's Giles Barnes. You'd better come over right away. We've got ghosts!"

Chapter 4

A Bad Case of Ghosts

"I'VE MADE SOME adjustments to the ghost-ometer," Tina told Giles. "I believe I've perfected it."

"She was up all last night working on it," said Kevin proudly. "She had to take apart the stereo for spare parts."

"Mom and Dad don't know yet," said Tina.

"Oh, yes they do," said Kevin. "Mom tried to play one of her Beatles CDs and it sounded like chipmunks."

"It can't be helped," said Tina. "This is important."

"Well, I hope you can figure this one out," said Giles, who'd been waiting for them outside in the front yard. "I was scared half to death."

"Oh, boy!" said Kevin. "Ghosts!"

"Kevin," said Tina, "be quiet. Now, Barnes, where did you see the ghosts?"

"You can call me Giles, you know."

"I prefer Barnes. Now, about the ghosts?"

"Well, I didn't exactly see them," Giles said. "I heard them. It was this weird fluttering sound, like birds' wings. And then I heard a voice, a woman's voice, say hello."

"A voice said hello?" Kevin asked. "That's all?"

"Yes."

"Oh," said Kevin disappointedly. "Doesn't sound very ghostly to me. No skeletons? No people without heads? No gushing —"

"Where did you hear these sounds?" Tina interrupted, giving her brother a withering look.

"In my bedroom." He told them how he'd heard the same sort of noise the very first night he'd arrived.

"Let us begin our investigation there, then," said Tina. "Lead the way."

Upstairs, they all stood very still and listened carefully.

"I don't hear a thing," said Kevin. "Are you sure you aren't making this up?"

"It was clear as anything!" Giles protested. "I heard it. It's not my fault if it's gone away now!"

"I am now going to take some readings with the ghostometer," Tina announced importantly.

She pulled the headphones over her ears and twirled some knobs. She listened intently for almost a minute, making little noises.

"Ahhhhh," she said, "hmmmmm . . . uh-huh . . . ohhhhh."

She took off the headphones and scribbled in a notebook.

"Well?" Giles demanded.

"Very interesting," said Tina.

"Aren't you going to tell us what you heard?" Kevin said.

"No."

"Why not?" blustered Giles.

"I need more information. It would be unprofessional of me to offer an analysis at this early stage."

Tina put the headphones back on and walked slowly around the room.

"She's awfully serious," Giles whispered to Kevin.

"She's a genius," Kevin whispered back. "Geniuses are supposed to be serious. It's a serious business. I'm serious sometimes, too, but since I'm only a little bit of a genius, I don't have to be as serious as Tina."

"I still think that thing looks like a toaster," Giles muttered, nodding at the ghostometer. "I bet it doesn't even work."

"Fascinating," Tina said to herself, jotting more notes into the book.

"Can we listen now?" Kevin inquired.

"No."

"Why not?" Giles demanded.

But Tina didn't say anything. It was as if she were in a trance. Finally she pulled off her head-phones and held them out to Kevin and Giles with-out saying a word. They clunked heads and shared the headphones.

Giles gasped. It wasn't just a simple fluttering of wings he heard this time, it was a symphony of bird sounds, chirping and whistling, cooing and squawking, hooting and warbling! And on top of all that was the clatter of beating wings! It was deafening. There must have been dozens of birds making all that racket!

Giles yanked off the headphones.

"Wow!" said Kevin.

"You mean all that's coming from my room?" Giles demanded, looking at Tina.

She was sitting silently on the edge of the bed, her hands folded neatly in her lap.

"Do you believe in ghosts?" she asked.

"I . . . I don't know," Giles stammered. "My mother says they don't exist. But my aunt Lillian believes in them. She says that —"

"Your room is haunted, Barnes," Tina said simply. "The readings on my ghostometer are unmistakable. You've got ghosts. You've got ghosts badly. It's the worst case of ghosts I've ever seen."

"It's also the first case of ghosts I've ever seen," Kevin added.

"But who's ever heard of ghost birds!" Giles blustered. "I mean —"

But he stopped suddenly. He stared. He pointed.

In the far corner of the room, on top of his bookshelves, was a large parrot. But it wasn't a real parrot. It was shimmering like a heat mirage. It was all silver and glittering, as if someone had drawn it in the air with sparklers. It strutted regally back and forth across the shelf, passing right through some of Giles's model planes.

Giles looked over at Tina, to make sure she was seeing it, too. She must have been. Her eyes were wide open. Kevin saw it, too. His mouth was wide open, but no words were coming out.

"It's . . . a ghost bird," Giles said.

"A ghost parrot, to be precise," said Tina.

"Hello!" said the parrot in a woman's voice. "Hello, hello!"

"Aha!" said Tina. "That explains the voice you heard."

And then, before Giles had time to speak, his entire bedroom was suddenly filled with ghost birds, all gleaming white, perched on the furniture, scratching on the desk, strutting around on the windowsill; there were birds chirping and singing and flying through the air. One swooped low toward Giles and he ducked, covering his head with his hands. The ghost bird soared right through him, but Giles didn't feel a thing, except a little buzz of static electricity in his head.

"The ghostometer readings are higher than ever before!" shouted Tina above the din.

"This is crazy!" shouted Giles. "My room is filled with ghost birds!"

"Can we go home now?" Kevin asked in a quavering voice.

Just as quickly as they'd come, all the ghost birds suddenly disappeared, and Giles's bedroom was back to normal. Except for a single silvery feather that floated slowly to the floor and stayed there for a moment before dissolving into empty air.

"It's extraordinary," said Tina. "I believe I counted over fifty different specimens."

"You actually counted them?" said Kevin in disbelief. "Weren't you afraid?"

"Fear is unscientific," said Tina.

"That's what my mother would say," said Giles miserably. "What am I going to tell my parents? They won't believe me. They'll think I've flipped!"

"Maybe you'd better let me have a chat with them," said Tina solemnly. "They might listen to me."

Chapter 5

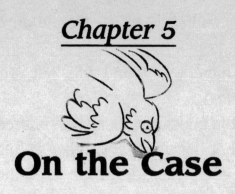

On the Case

"IT'S A PLEASURE to make your acquaintance, Mr. and Mrs. Barnes," said Tina Quark.

"Thank you, Tina," said Giles's father.

Giles saw that his parents were both smiling a little. They couldn't believe that such a tiny girl could be so serious. When Mr. and Mrs. Barnes had come home from shopping, Tina had asked them to please sit down at the dining room table.

"Now then," said Tina. "I realize that what I am going to tell you may be difficult to believe. But please try to keep an open mind. I have recently made an examination of your house and I've come to the conclusion that you have ghosts."

"I see," said Mr. Barnes. "Would anyone like a drink?"

"How have you found this out, Tina?" Mrs. Barnes asked.

"With the ghostometer," Kevin blurted out.

Tina shot her younger brother an incinerating glare. "Kevin, please, allow me to do the explaining here."

She lifted the ghostometer onto the table and showed it to Giles's parents.

"Mr. and Mrs. Barnes, this is a ghostometer, a personal invention of mine. It measures the amount of ghost activity, which human beings can't normally detect."

"It looks like a toaster," mumbled Mr. Barnes.

Tina pretended she didn't hear that.

"With this device, I have discovered a very high concentration of ghost activity in your son's bedroom."

"It's true," Giles told his parents. "We all saw them when you and Mom were out. We saw ghosts!"

"Now look," said Mrs. Barnes, getting into her stern professor mood, "I'm a woman of science myself, Tina, and I must tell you that what you're saying is preposterous, not to mention totally unscientific. . . ."

As Mrs. Barnes was speaking, Giles caught sight of something moving. He squinted. One of the ghost birds was swooping into the dining room from the hallway. It was the same regal parrot that Giles had seen in his bedroom.

"Um, Mom," said Giles, "there's —"

"Giles, please, let me finish," said his mother. "Now, I have never read a scientific account of ghosts that I have found satisfactory. . . ."

The ghost parrot fluttered through the room and perched on Mrs. Barnes's shoulder. Giles saw it. So did Kevin and Tina. So did Mr. Barnes. Mrs. Barnes, however, was too busy talking to take notice.

"Um, Mom," said Giles again.

"Giles, now let me — *aggggh!*" screamed Mrs. Barnes, finally seeing the bird on her shoulder. "Where did that come from?"

"It's what I've been trying to tell you, Mrs. Barnes," said Tina patiently. "You've got a bad case of ghosts — ghost birds, to be precise."

Mrs. Barnes was trying to shoo the ghost bird off her shoulder, but her hand just went right through it with a little buzzing sound.

"Well, Liz," Mr. Barnes said to his wife in a dazed voice, "it looks like Aunt Lillian was right."

"This is some kind of trick, isn't it!" Mrs. Barnes exclaimed. "All right, very funny, game's over."

"Mom, it's a real ghost!" Giles insisted. "There are dozens of them in my room. This house is haunted!"

Mrs. Barnes had her neck craned as far away from her shoulder as possible. She was staring into the eyes of the ghost bird, and the ghost bird was staring right back.

"Hello, hello!" said the parrot.

"There seems to be a parrot on my shoulder," she mumbled to herself.

"Where do they come from?" Mr. Barnes asked.

"Impossible to say," Tina replied calmly. "I'd have to research such a question very thoroughly before I could supply you with an adequate answer."

"Well, look," said Mr. Barnes. "This is completely unacceptable. We can't have ghost birds flying around our house. How can we get rid of them?"

"Another very good question, Mr. Barnes," said Tina. "Let me assure you that we'll get to work on it right away. In the meantime, I don't think there's any danger."

"Easy for you to say!" said Giles. "You don't have to sleep in my room! It's like an airport in there, all those birds swooping around my head!"

"Don't worry, we'll figure it out," said Kevin confidently. "After all, we *are* geniuses."

Chapter 6

Ghost Overload

"THERE ARE BIRDS in the bathroom now!" blustered Mrs. Barnes.

"Just try to ignore them," Mr. Barnes suggested. "They're perfectly harmless."

"There's no privacy in this house anymore!" Mrs. Barnes grumbled.

Giles couldn't help smiling. In the past two days, the ghost birds had taken over the entire house. They appeared and vanished without warning, sometimes one or two, sometimes dozens at a time. Most of them did seem to prefer Giles's bedroom, but it was not at all uncommon for a ghost cockatoo or a ghost budgie to turn up in the living room and roost on the television, or perch on a towel rack in the bathroom.

The regal ghost parrot seemed to have taken a special liking to Giles's mother and would often settle affectionately on her shoulder during meals or as she walked around the house.

"What a ridiculous creature," Mrs. Barnes would mutter, trying to shoo it away without success. "Won't this thing leave me alone?"

Giles's mother was not taking the ghostly invasion well at all. Giles knew that it was very hard for his scientific mother to admit that there really were ghosts living in their house and nibbling at her earlobes.

"We're not telling anyone about this," she instructed them. "I'd be the laughingstock of the mathematics department. Ghost birds! Hah!"

"Can't we even tell Aunt Lillian?" Giles wanted to know. "She'd be thrilled to see ghost birds."

"Absolutely not," said Mrs. Barnes. "She'd tell everyone she knew. She'd call the papers. We'd be on the six o'clock news. No. We tell no one."

As for Giles, he found he was gradually getting used to the ghost birds. He thought they were sort of beautiful, these sleek, silvery things, glittering with mysterious light. A few days later he discovered that you could make them disappear by blowing on them. They would flicker like a candle flame and then dissolve. But it was only temporary, and after a few minutes they would come back.

Often he could ignore the ghost birds altogether, but that wasn't always possible when they filled his room as if it were some giant cage, all shrieking and chirping and beating their wings. He'd started wearing earplugs in bed at night so he wouldn't be woken up by their early morning racket.

"When are we going to get rid of these things?" his mother roared that evening at the dinner table, puffing at every ghost bird that fluttered into view.

"Tina and Kevin are working on something," Giles said.

"They *are* geniuses," Mr. Barnes reminded his wife.

"Geniuses, right!" said Giles's mother. "I just hope they manage to clear these birds out of our house before I go crazy!"

Later that evening, Giles was sitting up in bed,

trying to read. A finch flew over and perched on the top of his book. Giles blew on it and it disappeared. He read another sentence and then an African swallow dive-bombed him.

"Hello, hello!" said the parrot, who suddenly decided to put in an appearance.

Giles laid his book down with a sigh. His room was overrun once again. Where did they all come from? He hoped that Kevin and Tina would cook up something fast. He wasn't sure how much more of this he could take!

All at once, Giles was aware of something else in the room with him.

Not a bird this time.

It was a person.

He turned his head to look. In the far corner of the room was an elderly woman. But, of course, she wasn't really a woman at all. She was all crackling light and electricity, just like the birds!

Giles sat rigidly in bed, watching her. It was one thing to see ghost birds, quite another to see the ghost of a real human being! Giles was certain the hair on his head was slowly rising. Was this the crazy lady Kevin had talked about?

But the ghost woman didn't take any notice of

him at all. She moved across the room, half walking, half gliding. She was looking carefully at the birds, stroking their plumage. She seemed upset, and Giles immediately felt sorry for her. She went from bird to bird, gazing at each one anxiously.

Then she turned and looked straight at Giles.

Giles felt his whole body go limp with fear. What's she going to do now? Giles wondered. All sorts of gory images flashed before his mind's eye. But the ghost woman just shook her head sadly. She had a kind face with plenty of wrinkles and silvery hair gathered on top of her head in a bun.

She raised a ghostly silver hand and pointed to the ceiling of Giles's bedroom. Then, taking one last look at the birds, she slowly faded from view until there was nothing left of her except a sprinkling of light hanging in the air, and that, too, disappeared after a moment.

First ghost birds, Giles thought, now a ghost woman.

What did it all mean?

Chapter 7

The Attic

"YOU MEAN THERE'S *another* ghost now?" Kevin exclaimed. "I think we're into ghost overload!"

"I haven't told my mom," said Giles. "She's getting pretty grumpy about the birds as it is. The strange thing is, the birds love her. There's a budgie that's been nesting on top of her head lately. It makes her furious. If I told her there was the ghost of a woman walking around, she'd go completely over the edge!"

"I bet it's the crazy lady everyone was talking about!" Kevin said enthusiastically. "Did she look crazy?"

"No, she didn't," said Giles. "She looked sad."

"Oh," said Kevin, disappointed.

Giles was trying to find a place to sit down in Tina and Kevin Quark's basement workshop, which was filled with old pieces of furniture and machinery. He settled on an upturned cardboard box.

"Dad and I called up Aunt Lillian in secret," he told the two Quarks. "And she said that ghosts are people who were very unhappy or upset when they died, and they keep on being unhappy for a long time afterward. So they wander around all sad, trying to figure things out."

"But what about all the birds?" said Kevin. "Who's ever heard of sad birds?"

"It's weird, I know," said Giles. "But the woman's obviously sad. And I think it has something to do with all the birds. They must have belonged to her. Listen to this. Remember how I told you the ghost lady pointed at the ceiling? Well, after I told Dad, I was wondering what it all meant. And I thought maybe she was pointing to the attic!"

"The attic!" said Kevin. "Now this is more like it! Did you go up?"

Giles nodded. "I didn't even know we had an attic. But Dad and I found a trapdoor in the ceiling. It pulled down with a little set of steps. We got some flashlights and climbed up. It was really dusty. Dad kept sneezing. But we found hundreds of old, empty birdcages in a big pile!"

"Hundreds, Barnes?" said Tina. "That sounds like somewhat of an exaggeration."

Giles rolled his eyes. "All right, not hundreds. But there were lots. I didn't count them. But who-ever this woman was, she must have had a lot of pet birds."

"Wow," said Kevin.

"Dad called up some of our neighbors, but none of them remembered who used to live in the house before us. Most of the people Dad talked to hadn't lived on the street that long. I wish I knew what happened."

"Yes, well," said Tina, looking up from a new gadget she'd been fiddling with, "I think we can give this a try."

"What is it?" Giles asked.

"It's great," said Kevin. "She took apart practi-cally everything in the house to make it — the ra-dio, TV, electric mixer. She's brilliant."

"Kevin —" said Tina.

"I know, I know," sighed her brother, "be quiet."

"Exactly. Now then, what I've been working

on is a device that should make the ghosts disappear for good. Stand back, everyone, please."

She flipped a little switch on the side of the contraption. There was a loud whirring noise, then a coughing, spluttering sound, and a big plume of yellow and black smoke curled up into the air.

"Well," said Tina. "That wasn't a huge success, was it?"

"Tina? Kevin?" a voice called down from the top of the stairs. "What's going on down there?"

"Nothing, Mom," said Tina.

"Don't worry," Kevin said to Giles, fanning smoke away from his face. "We'll come up with something. You won't have to live with ghosts for the rest of your life."

"Maybe we should try to find out more about the woman who used to live there," Giles suggested. "Maybe that would help."

Tina looked doubtful.

"It doesn't sound very scientific," she said.

"But it's a real mystery," Giles said. Something terrible must have happened. But what? If he knew that, maybe he'd be able to free his house from all the ghosts.

Chapter 8

Melanie Jones

ON HIS WAY HOME from the Quarks', Giles saw a man making his way down the street with the help of a walker, leaning heavily on the metal handles. Giles had seen him many times before. Every day at four o'clock he would shuffle very slowly down to the end of Stoker Street, then turn around and go back. It took him about forty-five minutes. But this evening, he stopped right in front of Giles's house.

"Hello," Giles said, walking up to him. "Can I help you?"

He thought at first that the man might be feeling sick. But now he saw that he was looking intently at the house, gazing straight up at his bedroom window.

"Oh, hello," the man said, still staring at Giles's window. "It's silly, isn't it, but I still expect to see birds in there."

Giles's heart thudded. "I'm sorry, what do you mean?" he asked, surprised. Could he know about the ghost birds, too? Had he seen them flying around?

"Melanie used to keep lots of birds. She had so many birds she barely knew what to do with them. Kept most of them in that room, right up there. I used to be able to see them when I took my walk."

"Did you know her?" Giles asked hopefully.

"Hardly at all," the man said. "No one really knew her. She barely put a foot out her door. Everyone thought she was a little batty, mind you, with all those birds. Poor Melanie Jones. It was a shame what happened. I only found out years later."

Giles waited patiently for him to continue.

"Bad heart," he said. "Melanie had a bad heart. I think they wanted to get her into one of those homes, but she wouldn't hear of it. She wouldn't have been able to look after those birds. But she had a heart attack one night, and they came and

took her to the hospital, but she never woke up. And there was no one to look after her birds. They all starved to death, poor things, before anyone thought to look in on them. It was sad, very sad."

"Oh," said Giles quietly. And suddenly everything clicked in his head. The ghost lady was Melanie Jones, coming back to take care of her poor, starved birds!

"I've just seen a lady ghost walk through the bathroom," said Mrs. Barnes, her face pale, as Giles rushed in the front door.

"It's the ghost of Melanie Jones," Giles said excitedly. "She's the one who lived here before us. She's the one who had all the birds!"

"Oh," said Mrs. Barnes. She hadn't blinked in quite a while.

"How did you find this out?" Mr. Barnes wanted to know.

"The man with the walker," Giles said, and he repeated the story he'd just heard outside.

"Well, that's just great," blustered Mrs. Barnes, who was beginning to recover from her shock. "But enough is enough. This is the last straw. There I was, getting ready for a nice hot shower, without budgies and bluejays, and just as I was about to step in, the ghost of Melanie Jones hustles through!"

"That's awful," said Mr. Barnes, trying to stifle his laughter.

"There's got to be laws about this kind of thing," muttered Mrs. Barnes. "Invasion of privacy by ghosts of various descriptions!"

The adoring ghost parrot chose that moment to settle on Mrs. Barnes's shoulder and nuzzle her ear affectionately.

"Hello, hello," it whispered.

Giles gave it a sharp blast of air.

"Awkkk," said the parrot as it disappeared.

"Oh, dear," said Mr. Barnes. "I have to admit, it's getting a little much. How are we supposed to lead a normal life? What about the Quarks? Have they figured something out?"

"Not yet," said Giles. "The last gadget Tina invented just went up in a puff of smoke."

What he didn't tell them was that he had an inkling of an idea of his own. He didn't want to say anything yet; he wasn't a genius, after all. He wanted to think it through. But maybe, just maybe, it would solve all their problems.

Chapter 9

The Plan

"I HAVE A PLAN," Giles announced the next day.

He'd called up Tina and Kevin and asked them to come right over, and now they were all sitting at the dining room table. His mother and father were there, too. So was the ghost parrot, and a squadron of budgies that were circling Mrs. Barnes's head and bombing her with ghost bird droppings.

Giles took a deep breath.

"Ghosts are usually very sad because something went wrong when they were alive. That's why they're still here, because they're trying to fix things up. Except that they can't because they're

dead. But they can't rest properly until they think everything's okay again."

"Who told you all this?" asked Mrs. Barnes.

"Aunt Lillian," Giles admitted.

"I won't listen. I don't believe a word that comes out of her mouth," Mrs. Barnes replied.

"That's what you said before you had a ghost parrot sitting on your shoulder," Mr. Barnes reminded her. "It won't hurt to listen, Elizabeth. Go ahead, Giles."

"Well, Melanie Jones keeps coming back because she's worried about all her birds. She must have loved them more than anything. She had dozens. But when she died they didn't have any food. So she couldn't feed them, and nobody else thought to feed them, so they starved to death."

He paused and looked around the table. Tina was looking at him very seriously.

"Maybe," Giles said, "if we feed the ghost birds, Melanie Jones will stop worrying and she won't feel so sad and all the ghosts will go away for good!"

There was a long silence.

"Barnes," Tina said, "do you have any idea how unscientific that sounds?"

"W-well . . ." he stammered.

"Those birds aren't real," Tina said. "They're ghosts. How could they eat anything?"

"Look," said Giles, "I know it sounds crazy, but it does kind of make sense. There's nothing any-body can do to change what happened, but maybe if we show Melanie Jones and the birds that we care, that'll be enough. Do you have a better idea?"

There was another long pause.

"No, I don't," Tina said. "My last gadget just burst into flames. And I don't think I'm going to be making any more for quite a while. Mom and Dad found out about the radio and the television —"

"And the electric mixer, and the frying pan," Kevin added. "Oh, and don't forget the *Encyclopaedia Britannica*. They weren't very pleased about that, either."

"Yes, it's been a bit of a disaster, really," said Tina, folding her tiny hands on the table. "We may have to shut down our genius business temp-orarily."

"Well," said Giles, "then we have no choice. We have to try my idea."

"All right," said Tina.

"I think I must be crazy, but I'm willing to try anything," muttered Mrs. Barnes, glaring at the parrot on her shoulder. "Let's get started."

Chapter 10

The Big Feed

"WE'D LIKE SIXTY-THREE pounds of your finest birdseed," said Giles.

"Sixty-three pounds," said the pet shop owner, looking at Giles as if this were all some huge practical joke. "That's an unusual amount of birdseed. Usually we sell these somewhat smaller boxes."

"No, that's not enough," said Tina Quark very seriously. "I've calculated our requirements exactly, and we need sixty-three pounds of birdseed."

"I see," said the pet shop owner, taken aback.

"And some of those birdie treats," said Kevin enthusiastically. "Yeah, they'll love those."

"Kevin —" Tina began.

"That's a good idea," said Giles, interrupting her. "We would also like twenty packs of birdie treats, please."

"You must have a lot of very hungry birds," said the pet shop owner nervously.

"Or one very large one," said Giles with a smile.

"Right," said the pet shop owner, hurrying off to fill the order.

Giles's parents were waiting for them outside in the car.

"I hope nobody saw us," muttered Mrs. Barnes as they drove off. "They'll think we're all loony. Sixty-three pounds of birdseed . . ."

Back home, Giles organized the preparations for the big feed. With Tina and Kevin's help, he brought down all the birdcages from the attic and began dusting and cleaning them. They polished the metal bars until they shone. They made sure the perches and roosts were firmly attached. They even put fresh newspaper at the bottom of each cage.

"They're just ghosts," muttered Mrs. Barnes. "Isn't this getting a little out of hand?"

"We have to do our best to show them we're sorry about what happened," Giles explained.

"I can't believe I'm doing this," said Tina. "It's so unscientific."

"Cheer up, Tina," said Kevin. "Who knows, maybe it'll work."

When all the cages were cleaned, they started filling the plastic feeding trays with seed from the huge sacks. They filled all the water bottles from the kitchen tap. And, for good measure, they hung birdie treats from the bars of every cage. Giles had prepared a bird feast the likes of which had never been seen in the animal kingdom.

"Now," said Giles, "let's set them all up in my room. That's where Melanie Jones kept them."

It took them a good half hour to carry all the cages upstairs and arrange them. By the time they were done, Giles's bedroom was absolutely crammed, filled wall to wall with birdcages. There were cages on every shelf, cages across the desk, on the windowsills, tall cages on pedestals standing side by side, cages on the bed and floor.

"If this works," said Mrs. Barnes, "I hope I never see another bird again as long as I live."

Suddenly a ghost bird appeared inside one of the cages. It sat on the perch, looking out at Giles, then noticed the tray of birdseed. It hopped over to the feeder and started eating.

"Here we go!" Giles exclaimed.

Then they came fast and furious. The ghost birds materialized so quickly that Giles couldn't keep track. They were filling up all the cages in his room, sometimes two or even three birds to a cage. And they were ravenous, gobbling seed, slurping water, gnawing at birdie treats.

"They're eating everything!" Giles shouted.

Except eating wasn't exactly the right word. The birds ate and ate, but the piles of food weren't getting any smaller. Still, it didn't seem to bother the birds. Giles lost track of time as the feast went on. But then, one by one, the ghost birds started disappearing.

First a budgie flickered out of sight.

Then a cockatiel vanished into thin air.

Then three finches evaporated in a puff of ghostly smoke!

"It's working!" Giles called out.

"I should have brought my ghostometer," Tina said.

"We don't need the ghostometer!" said Giles. "Can't you see it's working?"

The birds were blinking out like burned-out lightbulbs, faster and faster. As Giles watched, he felt a ghostly prickle move up his spine. He looked over his shoulder. The ghost of Melanie Jones had appeared among the cages.

"Look," Giles whispered, pointing.

"She's the one who interrupted my shower," mumbled Mrs. Barnes.

The ghost of Melanie Jones didn't look sad anymore; she was smiling, nodding and smiling as she watched her birds eating the best and biggest meal ever. Then she began to fade, faint and silvery, until there was nothing left. After that the rest of the ghost birds vanished with little pops of light until all the cages in Giles's room were finally empty.

"You must be a genius!" Kevin said to Giles. "You've done it!"

"It was completely unscientific," said Tina in a shaky voice, "and yet it seems to have been successful."

"Not completely," said Mrs. Barnes in a stern voice. "Look at this!"

The regal ghost parrot was perched on her shoulder.

"Hello, hello!" it said.

"No, look, it's fading, too!" said Giles.

"Good-bye, good-bye," said the parrot, and, with a little puff of light, it was gone.

"Well, that's a relief," said Mrs. Barnes.

"You looked pretty good with a parrot," said Mr. Barnes, hugging his wife.

"Well, they're all gone now," said Giles, gazing at the empty cages. Strangely, the house seemed too quiet, and he felt a twinge of sadness. He hadn't realized it, but he'd become rather fond of the birds, and all their noise and activity. The ghosts had kept him so busy he hadn't even had a chance to miss his old friends. In fact, he'd made some new ones. Maybe the summer wouldn't be so bad after all.

"What are we going to do with all that seed?" Mr. Barnes said.

"And the cages?" asked Mrs. Barnes.

"Maybe," Giles said with a smile, "we should get some birds."